ABCEDAR

An Alphabet of Trees

by George Ella Lyon
designed and illustrated by Tom Parker

Orchard Books / New York

A B C D E F G H I J K L M

Orchard Books, 95 Madison Avenue, New York, NY 10016

Manufactured in the United States of America
Printed by Barton Press, Inc. Bound by Horowitz/Rae
The text of this book is set in Futura Extra Bold.
The illustrations are india ink with photo-mechanically applied colors.

Hardcover 10 9 8 7 6 5 4 3 2
Paperback 10 9 8 7 6 5 4 3 2 1

Library of Congress Cataloging-in-Publication Data
Lyon, George Ella, date.
A B Cedar: an alphabet of trees / by George Ella Lyon;
designed and illustrated by Tom Parker.
Summary: An alphabet book introducing the leaves from a variety of trees.
ISBN 0-531-05795-X (tr.)   ISBN 0-531-08395-0 (lib. bdg.)
ISBN 0-531-07080-8 (pbk.)
1. Trees—Identification—Juvenile literature.   2. Leaves—Identification—
Juvenile literature.   3. English language—Alphabet—Juvenile literature.
[1. Trees—Identification.   2. Leaves—Identification   3. Alphabet.]
I. Parker, Tom, ill.   II. Title.
QK477.2.I4L96 1989   582.16—dc19   [E]
88-22797

NOPQRSTUVWXYZ

In memory of my grandfather, J.D. Fowler, who knew trees,
and Jamie Duke, who loved letters.

G.E.L.

A B C D E F G H I J K L M

A stand of trees

ABCEFGHIJKL

A million billion leaves

each season from

NOPQRSTUVW XYZ

HICKORY   IRONWOOD

JUNIPER

KUMQUAT

P O P L A R   Q U I N C E

A B C D E _ G H I J K L M

REDBUD   SASSAFRAS

ABCDEFGHIJKLM

UMBRELLA TREE

VELVET ASH

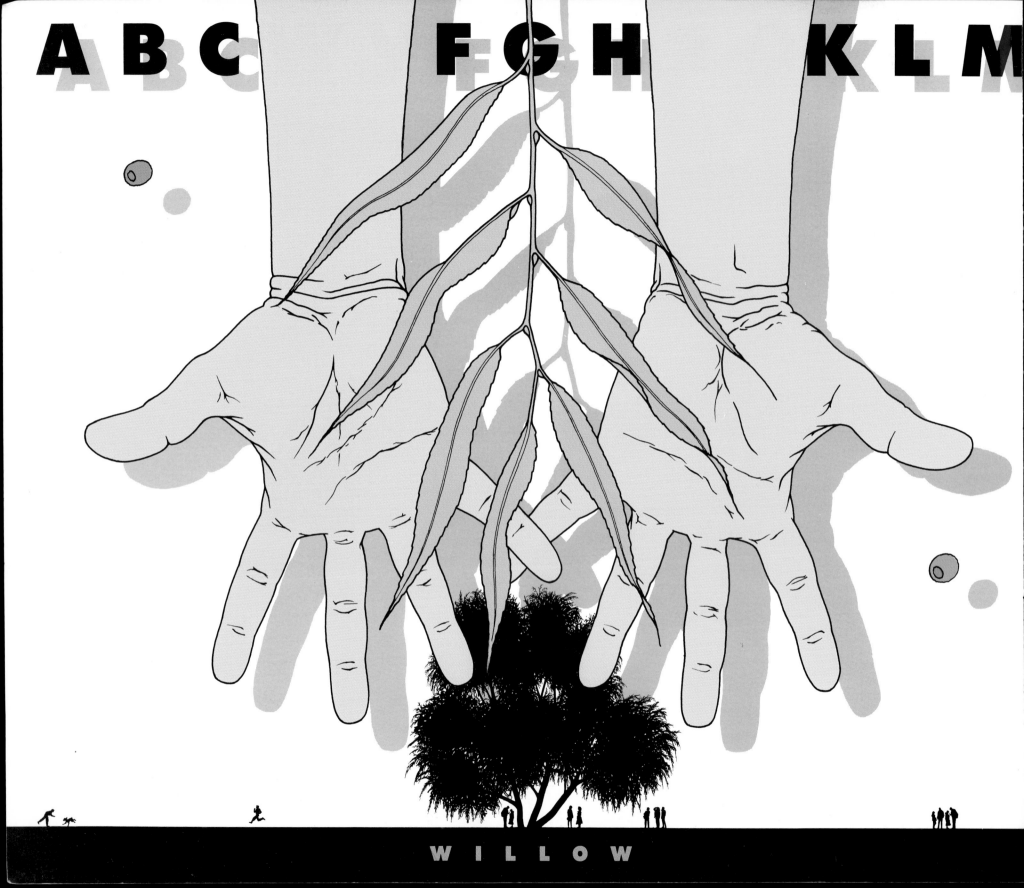

A B C   F G H   K L M

WILLOW

ABCDEFGHIJKLM

Air and food   Shade and wood

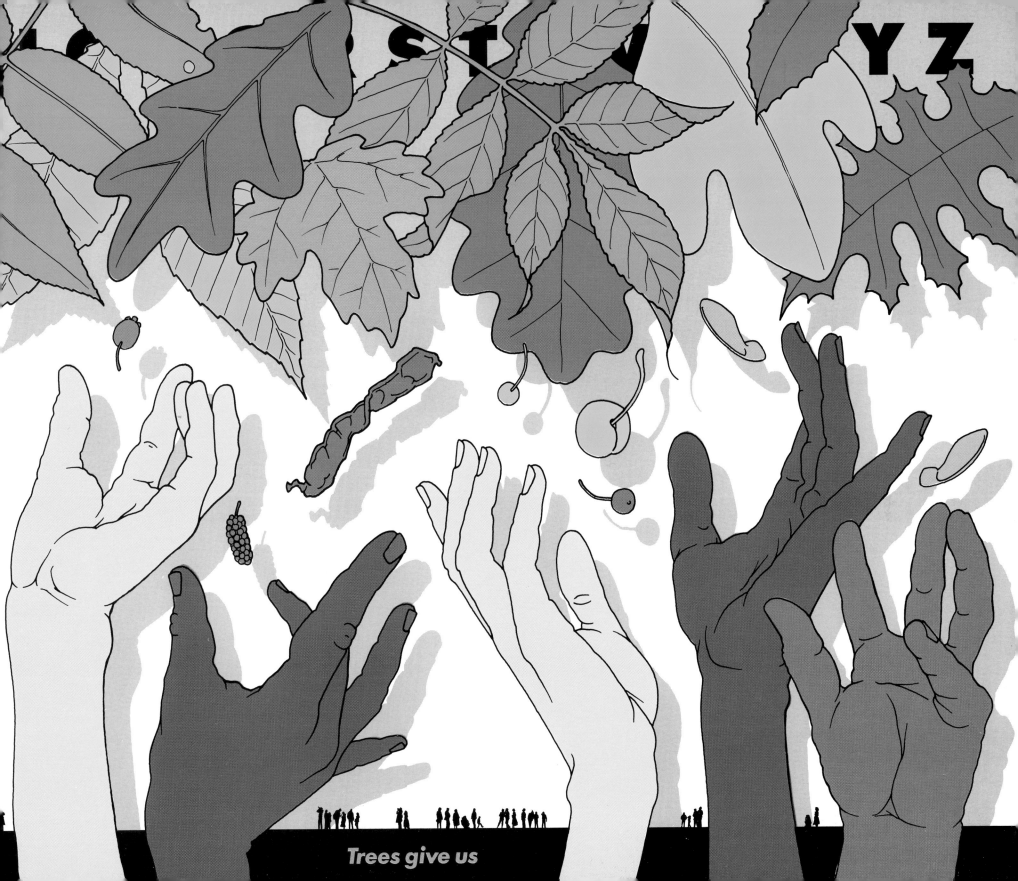

Trees give us

Even this book!